For Valerie, Christine, Dominique, Cora, and Hazel.
With all my love, hugs, and kisses.
And for Alessia, the real *Hugga Loula*.

Text copyright © 2021 by Nancy Dearhorn
Illustration copyright © 2021 by Huang Junyan
All rights reserved.

Published by Familius LLC, www.familius.com
1254 Commerce Way, Sanger, CA 93657

Familius books are available at special discounts for bulk purchases, whether for sales promotions
or for family or corporate use. For more information, email orders@familius.com.

Reproduction of this book in any manner, in whole or in part, without written permission of the publisher is prohibited.

Library of Congress Control Number: 2020947678

Print ISBN 9781641702713
Ebook ISBN 9781641704908
KF: 9781641705141
FE: 9781641705349

Printed in China

Edited by Kaylee Mason and Brooke Jorden
Cover and book design by Carlos Guerrero

10 9 8 7 6 5 4 3 2 1

First Edition

Hugga Loula lay on her bed reading a book. She heard a terrible racket coming from the garage.

It was the crashing and clashing of Dad's tools.
Hugga Loula raced to the garage.

Dad was muttering angry words under his breath.
"What's wrong?" Hugga Loula asked.
Dad's tools were scattered all over the floor, and he was searching through
them. "I need . . . I need . . ."

Before Dad could finish his sentence, Hugga Loula said,

"If you're grumpy or sad, frustrated or mad,
just give a shout, and hug it out."

Then she wrapped her arms around him, and Dad's anger evaporated into thin air. "Thank you," he said. "I was going to say my slip-joint pliers, but a hug is what I really needed."

Hugga Loula searched through Dad's tools, found his pliers, and helped Dad tighten those bolts with a **CLINK CLINK**. Then she returned to reading her book.

Hugga Loula had just settled in again when she heard a commotion coming from the kitchen. It was the clanging and banging of Mom's pots and pans.

Hugga Loula hurried
to the kitchen.

Mom was mumbling under her breath.
"What's wrong?" Hugga Loula asked.
"I guess I'm a little stressed out," Mom said.
Pots and pans were scattered all over the kitchen counter.
Mom was searching through them.
"I need . . . I need . . ."

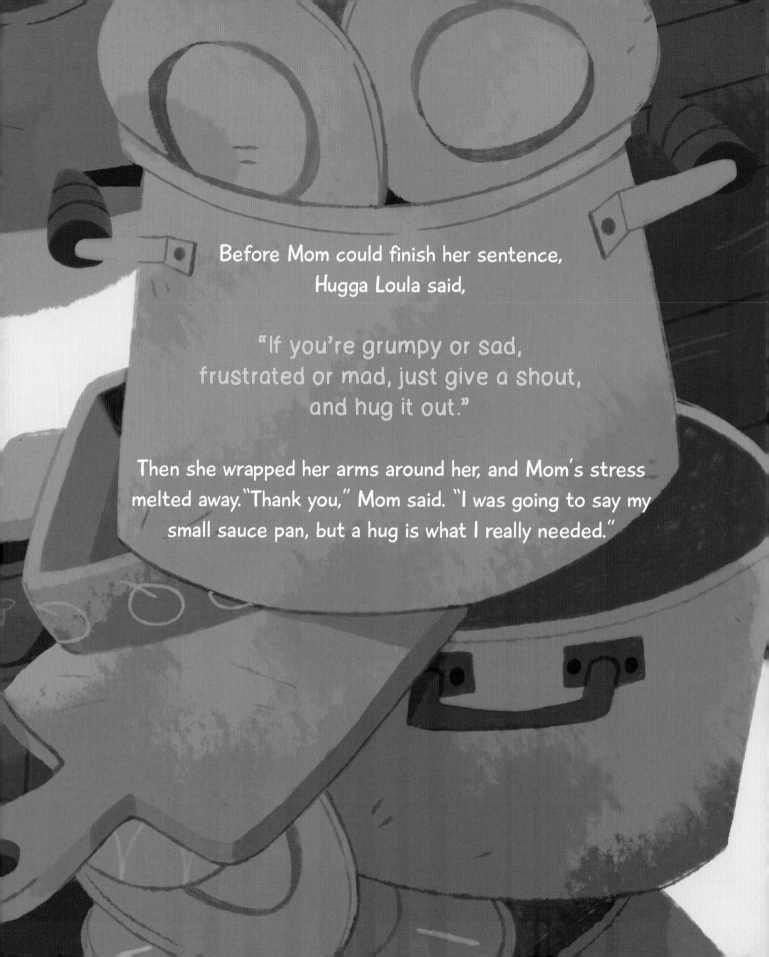

Before Mom could finish her sentence,
Hugga Loula said,

"If you're grumpy or sad,
frustrated or mad, just give a shout,
and hug it out."

Then she wrapped her arms around her, and Mom's stress
melted away. "Thank you," Mom said. "I was going to say my
small sauce pan, but a hug is what I really needed."

Hugga Loula searched through Mom's pots and pans, found the small sauce pan, and helped Mom make soup with a STIR STIR. Then Hugga Loula returned to reading her book.

Hugga Loula had just settled in again when she heard a ruckus coming from her brother's bedroom.

It was the bumping and thumping of Steve's toys.
Hugga Loula set down her book and rushed to his room.

Tears ran down Steve's cheeks.
"What's wrong?" Hugga Loula asked.
His toys were scattered all over the floor,
and he was searching through them.
"I need . . . I need . . ."

Before Steve could finish his sentence, Hugga Loula said,

"If you're grumpy or sad, frustrated
or mad, just give a shout, and hug it out!"

Then she wrapped her arms around him, and Steve's sad
frown turned upside down. "Thank you," he said. "I was going
to say my favorite truck, but a hug is what I really needed."

Hugga Loula searched through Steve's toys, found his favorite truck, and handed it to him with a VROOM VROOM.

Then she returned to reading her book.

Hugga Loula had just settled in again when Dad, Mom, Steve, and her dog, Lorenzo, appeared at her bedroom door.
Dad cleared his throat. "You calmed and comforted us with your hugs, so we wanted to give you something in return."

They all wrapped their arms around Hugga Loula and gave her the biggest, super-duperest group huddle hug ever!

If you're grumpy or sad, frustrated or mad,
just give a shout, and hug it out!

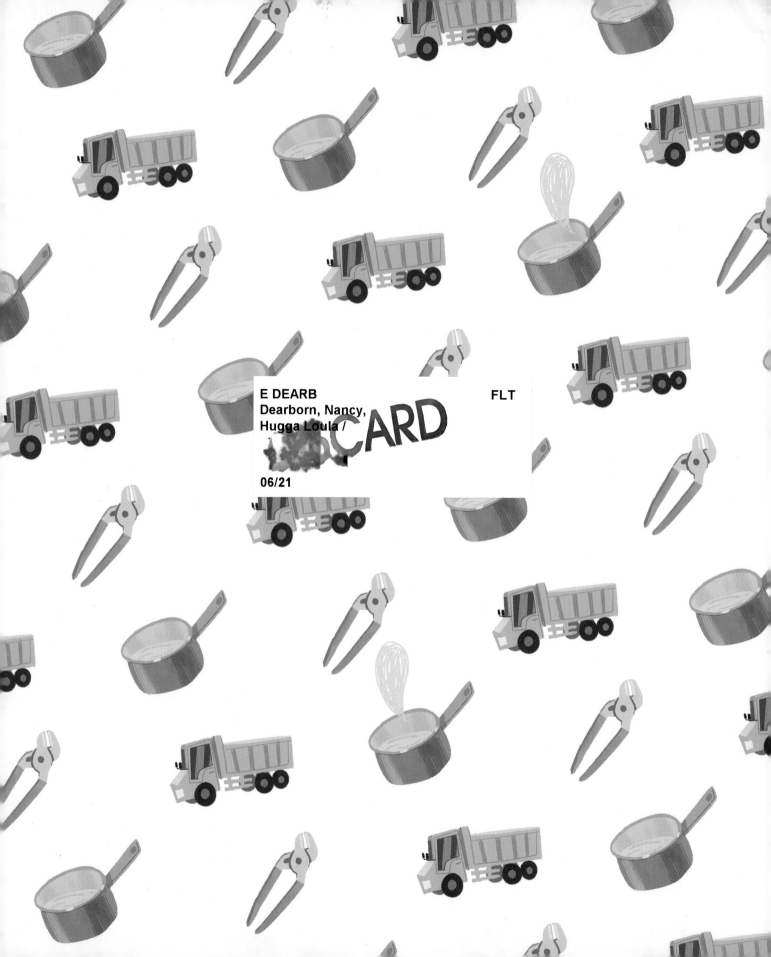